Alishia

I hope you enjoy this
story as much as I
enjoyed writing it!

Enjoy the journey! ♡

J. Rokate

One Door Closes

THE BEGINNING

J. Roberts

One Door Closes: The Beginning

©2023, J. Roberts

ISBN: 978-1-66789-584-0

ISBN eBook: 978-1-66789-585-7

To my Father, my Al:

The answers were never important to me.

I only asked questions so I could hear you speak.

Your wisdom will be etched into my heart forever...

In this lifetime, the ones that came before it,
and all lifetimes yet to come.

To the lost ones:

The wanderers. The ones who never felt "normal."
The ones who never quite "fit in." The ones who feel uneasy
amongst the masses and at home beneath the trees.
The ones who find themselves asking "why."

This is for you.

NEW MEXICO

Present Day

The mirror. What a confusing and wasteful instrument! There's always been such a disconnect between what it shows us and how we see ourselves. But for some reason, today, it tells the truth. It's one thing to look at your reflection and have no idea who is staring back at you; it's another completely to recognize the lines you see as a way to retrace every step you've taken through the years. They are marionette strings set beside your lips, retelling stories of the times you laughed until you cried. The crow's feet nestled into the sides of your eyes tell tales of a life of wonder, mystery, of hard-earned wisdom. It's always been a matter of perspective, I suppose. I can remember a time when the mirror was my enemy.

As a woman in my seventies, you would think I'd be disappointed with the person staring back at me, but the truth is, I still feel twenty-five. I'm not sure if it's the strange events that have occurred in my life that have granted me the fortune of feeling young still, or if that's just how it should be. What I do know is that if I didn't pass by a mirror every now and then, I'd hardly know I was aging. I do find myself wondering occasionally how long my body will be able to keep up with my mind, though.

But for now, on the morning of this hike up Wheeler Peak, I've still got what it takes to make it to the top. I don't have a choice, really. Not just because Lucy invited me, but because there's a beckoning within me, a voice even, telling me that this is where I need to be. And, maybe even after all this time, the voice is his. All I know is that I need to find out.

When I met Lucy, fifty years ago, it's fair to say we were very different people than we are now, or at least I was. Lucy's eccentricity was always the antithesis of what I was brought up to be, but, in the end, our shared experience bonded us. After all, it was she who led me to the start of my journey and she's always been the encouraging type, to put it mildly.

Now it's no surprise that all these years down the road she's invited me to speak at one of her retreats. She thinks I've gained a reputation for making people think beyond the realm of possibility, but I just know what I know, and I know what I've seen, and it's only one in every hundred people who actually hear what I'm saying anyway. My entire life's work has been one of constant skepticism, but I guess the beauty of knowing oneself is that the doubts of others don't cast a shadow on the truth that lives inside you.

"Jo! Are you ready to get going? The students are waiting!" Interrupting my thoughts was that cheerful, singsong voice I've always loved.

"All set, Lu, let me just get my bag."

As I turned around to acknowledge her, all I could see was the back of her, skipping out of the room. I couldn't help but laugh. *Nimble as ever, even at her age.* After all these years, she never stops surprising me. I took one last sip of my coffee before grabbing my things, making sure to savor the taste and that freshly caffeinated smell one last time before embarking on the hike.

As I stepped outside, I was suddenly met by the very confused gazes of a group of students. Based on the expressions on their faces, they were only waiting for Lucy. It struck me at that moment that she hadn't told them about me joining them at all. A knowing chuckle escaped my lips, which I'm sure only puzzled them more.

Speaking of Lucy, where is she? It's just like her telling me to hurry and not be ready herself.

As if she could hear my thoughts, there she was, bounding through the doorway, lips curved in a Cheshire-cat grin, humming something to the tune of, *I have a plan that I haven't clued you in on.* If I know her as well as I think I do, all will be revealed in time, so it's best just to follow her lead where that's concerned.

Without another word or explanation to the group about who I am, or why it's necessary to have not just one but two members of the elderly community with them on this retreat, we are off. Two old women and a handful of doctoral candidates on their way to the top of the highest peak in New Mexico, carrying nothing but our bags, our ambition, and, for me, a little voice that told me something was waiting for me along the journey.

Fortunately, the hike is only a few hours today, as we will be stopping at William's Lake to picnic and then go a mile or two more before ultimately setting up camp for the evening and then heading to the peak tomorrow. I may still have my wits and my health, but I'm not quite sure I can manage a hike of this magnitude in only a day. We've started north of the Taos ski basin, giving us a bit of an advantage with distance and the opportunity to see some of the most extraordinary views along the way. I find myself secretly hoping our companions can appreciate it, as I remember this trek from long before it was used for tourism and it was even more glorious then. *It's always a shame to waste views on those who move through life with their eyes closed.*

The air is cool enough that you can faintly see the breath as it leaves your lips, which, of course, is a good reminder that you're still breathing at this elevation. If you close your eyes for just a moment and focus, the smell of cedar and fir fills the rest of your senses; you can almost picture the scenery without even having to look.

The six students trekking on ahead of us are more than eager to get this over with I'm sure, but these trips are something that's required of them before starting their program at Cambridge. Each of them has been hand-selected by Lucy for this specific outing, so they'll have to endure it whether they want to be here or not. You can feel the tension in them, the anticipation of what's coming, the anxiety of what this all means for their future as history doctoral candidates.

It's a feeling I remember vividly, though one I would rather not recall. Perhaps their anxiety comes from a sense of confusion about what they are actually doing here and why they were chosen specifically. But of course, as it always is with Lucy, there's a reason. I'm beginning to suspect what my involvement is.

"Jo, maybe you can get ahead of me a bit and start chatting with some of the students. I'm sure they're eager to know who you are." She was exasperating.

I let out a small laugh. "Lu, you're something else. Do you really think this is going to work?"

Lucy doesn't pause often, but at this question, she stops dead in her tracks and narrows her eyes at me. "I knew what was going to work back then, didn't I?"

Taking the hint, I pick up my pace and head toward the student closest to me. As I attempt to catch up, albeit slowly, I can't help but look down as I'm reminded of the familiar feeling underfoot. There's a wonderful ruggedness to the terrain, even though it's been well worn by travelers now, which brings me back to the first moment I stepped into these woods.

The first person I came to was a very tall young man, caramel-colored skin with short dark hair, rounded glasses, and a deep look of concentration in his eyes. It took me about two seconds to assess that he meant business about the program and that perhaps it was a very good thing he was here. And I could tell all that without having any conversation.

I decided to loudly point out some of the native wildlife to see if I could get his attention that way, as the entire time we'd been matched for pace he hadn't even looked over or seemed to notice I was there. I exaggerated a gasp and exclaimed, "Ooohh, a Pinyon Jay! Just gorgeous aren't they?" That seemed to startle him, as his head whipped around to face me suddenly.

"Oh my! I'm so sorry, I had no idea someone was standing next to me!"

I smiled. "Yes, it seems you were incredibly focused! That's not a bad thing.'"

"I suppose not." He stopped walking, and I noticed a look of frustration sweep across his face.

"I'm just trying to get this hike over with as soon as possible. All I can think about is my thesis, and if I'm out here I'm not working on my research."

"Ahhh, yes, the infamous thesis. It makes sense you'd want to get back to your more typical methods, but what if I told you that this trip is research?"

He cocked his head to the side and let out an arrogant laugh. "Well, I'd have to say I'm not sure hiking in New Mexico is going to help me find out about the Construction of the Danube Monarchy."

"Maybe not, Mr. … ?"

"Desh. Rohan Desh."

"Right. Well, maybe not, Mr. Desh. But have you ever thought about what you'll do with your degree when your thesis is done? When the research is over and the constant stress of having to complete this program has subsided?"

He looked at me, slightly bewildered, and all I could do was smirk.

"Will you teach? Will you curate? How will you teach? What will you collect?" I stopped walking abruptly and gestured toward the familiar pine-covered peaks in front of us.

"The truth is, Mr. Desh, there's a whole world outside of your dissertation that is steeped in the history you claim to love. Try looking up from your feet for just a moment, and you might see it."

I couldn't quite decipher from the look in his eyes if I'd just said something he considered revolutionary, or if he wanted to hit me with his walking stick. He narrowed his eyes. "Who are you, exactly?" he asked me with a slight air of annoyance.

I chuckled and smiled at him coyly before responding, "You can call me Jo."

And just like that, we were back to silently striding beside each other until, as I expected, he started to outpace me. I started to think again about my purpose here, knowing inherently that there is always a reason for where we are. I know Mr. Desh isn't the one I'm here to find. But if there's anything my life's work has taught me, it's not to count out the stubborn ones. I used to be one of them, after all.

My eyes drift upward to the view between the pines: dappled sunlight and lush green stretching out as far as I can see. I think back to being in my late twenties, much like Mr. Desh, a time when my eyes never saw anything except the inside of a book; books that told me where to look, but not how to see. It's difficult to reflect on all the years I spent clouded by my ambition because life is so different now. It has been, ever since that rainy day on the cobblestone streets of England.

Standing on these hills, breathing in the scent of the same clay humans dug in hundreds of years ago, my hands begin to ache. You'd think my age would cause this throbbing in my hands, but no, it's longing. Longing to dig, to make, to be one again with this place. In this moment, I realize I have truly come full circle. That moment of clarity affords me another answer. *I know why she's brought me here. She wants me to tell them the story.*

All I can hear from behind me is exaggerated breaths mixed with the sound of a walking stick hitting the ground unnecessarily hard, and I realize I must've slowed down quite a bit whilst stuck in my thoughts, as it's obvious Lucy has caught up to me.

"So, you've figured it out then?" she asks, grinning and breathless as she makes her way to my side.

I put one hand on her back and stop to let her catch her breath. "How do you always know what I'm thinking?"

"You aren't the only one who has gifts, you know," she replies with a wink.

She turns her head for a quick moment, as if to collect her thoughts. When she looks back up to meet my gaze, I can see that something in her has shifted. Her unequivocal glee has morphed into a sternness, a seriousness that I know is rare coming from her. Without ever releasing her eyes from mine, she reaches down and grabs my hand.

"It's time, Jo. I promised him that in my lifetime I would see you through this transition. The one you're looking for is here."

Knowingly, I nod my head and give her hand a gentle squeeze. Before I can even register what she's said, she takes off, walking stick in hand, gleeful stride rightfully back in place.

The hike to the lake is taking a bit longer than originally thought, not in the least due to the fact that Lucy and I are about a half-mile behind the students. She never brings up the topic again, just goes on for a while about how excited she is for the students to be here and how bright they all are. I realize how incredible it is that after all these years her enthusiasm has never wavered, how she seems to have been born with an innate quality to find the best in people. It's that exact quality that always made me wonder why I was chosen and she wasn't. If I'm honest with myself, though, I know the answer. She was chosen for a different job entirely.

After another hour, we were met with the most glorious view of the Sangre De Cristo Mountains canopied by lush forest and the faintest brushstrokes of clouds dotting the peaks. William's Lake opens out in front of us and welcomes us with open arms. While I am always glad for the scenery, right now I'm exceptionally grateful for the chance to sit down. The students are already there, down by the water, unpacking their bags, setting out their food and notebooks.

Lucy and I slowly make our way to meet them before taking out our blankets and promptly sitting down for a well-deserved rest. With my bottom barely on the ground, a female voice bellows from the group. "Professor, are we doing our lecture before we eat or after?" she asks.

Lucy raises her eyebrows and gives a wicked smile before replying to the girl. "Both."

I couldn't help but laugh. Same old Lucy, never making it easy.

I watch her rise again, a bit unsteadily, from the ground and begin to dig furiously into her bag for something. Of course, as she's not told me of her plans, I can only imagine what she has in store for them. She took out a small plastic bag, and out of it came six small burlap sacks.

"The first step is for each of you to take one of these and put it in your bag immediately. The second step is for you to not open them until I say so." I raise an eyebrow as I watch her pass them out to each student one by one, making sure they put them away quickly, fervently attempting to dodge any questions about the contents. I'm curious, of course, but unlike them, I know her. There's a reason for whatever is in there.

She makes her way back to her blanket and addresses them once again. "I know you have all been wondering who this lovely lady sitting to my right is and why she is on this retreat with us. This is my longtime friend, colleague, and researcher of ancient history, Dr. Josephine Pearce." A small gasp escapes the lips of one of the students and I realize it belongs to Mr. Desh. I grin, meeting his surprised expression with my own amused one, knowing in that moment he knows exactly who I am. It was humorous, really, to think he probably thought two hours ago I was just an old lady who wanted to hike. The truth is, though, I'm that too.

"I've brought her here today because she has spent her career giving a very different perspective about how to go forward, not just in this chosen field of study but in life, to many people. And I think her story will help you all on your journey forward."

In my heart, I knew that was why she brought me here: my story. I only hope that, after hearing it, at least one of them can connect to it, that at least one of them has a flicker of something other than disbelief in their eyes afterward.

I take a deep breath before I begin and close my eyes to ground myself. The wind picks up suddenly and the air between the pines starts to whistle. I feel recognizable electricity through my body and I know he is with me. It's time.

"Thank you very much for the introduction, Professor Dawes. You can all call me Jo as, fortunately for you, I am not your teacher, just an old woman with a lot of experience and a lot of stories. We can start with why you are all here. History. Can anyone give me the definition of it?"

A familiar hand shoots up from the group. I gesture for Rohan to go ahead and answer the question.

"History is a collection of facts about the past," he says smugly.

I let out a small chuckle, which only seems to annoy him, before offering my reply. "It can be simply defined as the events of the past and the hows and whys of what occurred when, but in my experience, it's more than that. It's intrinsic, knowing that everything that happened before you is connected to you. And to be a successful student in this field requires you to possess a perpetual hunger to know more. It demands that curiosity be sewn into the very fiber of your being and that your mind be as open and as vast as the scenery before you."

"But history is a collection of facts!" a very frustrated voice interrupts.

"Okay then, Mr. Desh, you have the floor. Go on."

"It's facts, things that can't just be changed. History has happened, and the proof is concrete. It's not philosophical. Haven't you made your career by just hypothesizing about historical events, instead of actually researching them?"

I smile softly at him, knowing he's not entirely incorrect. It's what I'm most widely known for: I'm the crazy history researcher who published papers about historical happenings without any concrete proof or explanation.

"I have, in fact, made my career out of disrupting the norm in this field. I won't pretend my teachings went without doubt from my peers. On the contrary, there have always been more skeptics than believers."

"You see, what traps us, and what held me back for so long from experiencing this subject in its true form, is ourselves. It's a sense of rushing for results instead of experiencing them. It's fear of how we are perceived, fear of the unknown, and fear of failure. It's the human tendency to push away curiosity in the name of logic and rational thinking instead of embracing child-like qualities of imagination and wonder and becoming deaf to all of the voices that whisper inside us."

"History is just that. It's a collection of people and events that required those infantile instincts of curiosity and bravery, resulting in some of the best and worst that humanity has to offer. History is not learning of the things that occurred before you. It's knowing. And it's knowing that you are tied more closely to all of it than you ever realized."

"Are there any questions so far?" I ask reluctantly, knowing simply by the look in their eyes and them feverishly writing down what I said that most of them were treating this as if there would be a pop quiz at the end, instead of simply listening, absorbing. I also know by looking at Mr. Desh's narrowed eyes, basically burning a hole through my head, that he has something to say … again. He raises his hand.

"You wrote a paper in 1980 about the dwellings and living conditions at Stonehenge. You spoke of traditions and in detail of the inhabitants, the stones, and their purpose. It was as if you knew exactly what happened, when people had spent hundreds of years theorizing and disproving those theories. Yet you wrote about it as if it were fact and never provided any evidentiary support."

"Is that a question or a comment, Rohan?" I ask, amused. Yet, he still looked at me, waiting for an answer. I quietly wonder how long he has wanted to say that.

"It was something I just knew. It was something I experienced. I think you'll be delighted to know that I'm about to tell the story of how I happened upon those answers, among many others, momentarily."

Another hand goes up in the group. This time it's the young girl directly to my right who I've not yet spoken to and, regretfully, have hardly noticed until now. "You say we have to experience history. How do we do that? How do we get to that point?"

I turn my head to look at her, but just as the words are about to come out of my mouth, I'm struck by something very familiar. There's something about her I feel I've seen many times before. *Perhaps it's a sadness in her eyes.* I shake myself from the distraction and muster up my answer. "Good question. What's your name, dear?"

"Cara McCarthy."

"Well, Cara," I say, matching her gaze, "in order to address your question completely, I'd have to tell you all a story I've never spoken about before now."

I could feel the intensity in Lucy's energy rise, as if she had been living for this very moment.

"And to do that I have to follow the advice a very wise man once gave me, and start at the beginning."

Lucy lays back on her blanket with her bedroll underneath her, her hands clasped behind her head. She closes her eyes gently, with a smile and thinks to herself, Ahh yes, the beginning. But whose?

CAMBRIDGE UNIVERSITY

England

1980

T HUMP!

The doors to the auditorium closed and shook me back to reality. I stood at the podium and scanned my eyes over seats that were full just moments ago. The room was empty now, and so was I.

This research, this presentation. It was supposed to be the pinnacle of my career. A highlight if there ever was one. I should have been celebrating my accomplishment right now. Instead, I found myself gripping my notes in my hand, information that had taken me almost ten years to collect mind you, and crumbling it aggressively before shoving it into my bag. *The Importance of Preservation in Ancient Civilizations.* Ha.

It should really be called, "The importance of not being so damn boring that no one even claps after they hear you speaking for two hours."

The moment keeps replaying in my mind like a broken record. I'd clicked over to the last slide of the presentation, said, "Thank you for your time," and waited for a round of applause that never came. I was greeted, instead, by a few polite claps—likely those who were apparently glad it was finally over—and the backsides of the students leaving the lecture hall. I thought I would feel accomplished when it was over, as if somehow all the work I'd done would be earth-shattering and profound. But about halfway through hearing myself repeat fact after fact after fact, the monotony overcame me. And I felt empty when it was over. Not excitement, not pride … nothing. *And, apparently, the students agreed.*

I knew I needed to make my way out for the next lecturer, but I couldn't move from the podium. Flashbacks from grad school started playing in my mind like a film reel as I continued to stare blankly at the back of the hall. I was always the first to raise my hand, the first to finish every test, even finished first in my class, damnit. Yet there I was, the complete opposite of what I'd always believed myself to be. This should have been a proud moment for me. I was a woman, with a doctorate, standing on one of the most prestigious academic stages of the world, yet I felt completely void of any real accomplishment.

I don't quite remember how I convinced my feet to move from that stage, but somehow, I did. I threw my bag over my shoulder, and the next thing I knew I was putting one foot in front of the other and making my way down the steps toward the exit.

My mind was swirling with thoughts, and I couldn't decipher one from the other. I could only hear my feet dragging on the worn red carpet that ran down the center of the aisles as I felt the clamminess in my hands start to build. As I reached the doors to leave, I took a look back at the stage. The emptiness of the room perfectly reflected how I felt.

In the back of my mind echoed the voice of my mother. I could practically see her pursed lips and hear the bitterness in her tone.

You should get a real job like your brother, Jo.

History doesn't pay bills, Jo.

If you're not going to be a doctor or a lawyer, then at least be a good housewife, Jo.

She always thought I was crazy to enter this profession, especially as a woman. Instead of being proud that I'd broken certain barriers to be there, she loved to remind me that it was much more suitable for me to be at home with my husband and kids, instead of chasing some silly dream. I love my husband and children, of course, but I never thought I would have to choose. I wanted my daughters to see that I could do both. I never wanted them to think their dreams were out of reach. But in that moment, I couldn't help but feel like maybe she was right … maybe I'd been so caught up in the fantasy of being accepted into this world that I never realized I wasn't very good at it. *I'll never tell her she was right.*

I collected myself quickly, just enough to look away and push open the double doors. Somehow, they were heavier now than they were this morning. I walked quickly toward the bathroom, as I could feel the tears welling into pitiful pools beneath my eyelids. I may have failed, but I was determined not to let anyone else see that I knew it.

I'm pretty sure that anyone watching me thought I had serious stomach issues by the way I ran in there. I didn't even notice how aggressive I must have been until I pushed the bathroom door open and the sheer force made it slam into the wall. I got to the nearest sink and dropped my bags at my feet. The only thing I could think to do was turn the water on to the coldest setting and splash my face until I couldn't tell the difference between tears and water. I thought maybe it would ground me a bit, bring me back to reality. I stood, gripping the sink on both sides, panting with angst, begging myself to get a grip, but I could only look up.

Mirrors. What a confusing and wasteful instrument. As if what I need is to see the physical manifestation of how I feel.

Bloodshot eyes and blotchy cheeks, all hints of color drained from my face. It was in this moment that I realized I had no idea who I was. Outside of my career and my family, my identity was null, at least to me. I needed something more than a miracle to pull me out of it.

Suddenly the bathroom door swung open behind me, and jaunting in came a very frantic, tiny woman with black, untamed, frizzy hair, and glasses … like something out of a Tolkien novel, but with a huge grin on her face. I recognized her instantly as Dr. Dawes, the eccentric history professor I'd heard so much about

ONE DOOR CLOSES: THE BEGINNING

from my peers. After hearing about how much they tried to avoid her, I will admit I was a bit scared by her presence.

"Sorry to startle you, love, gotta pee! Don't mind me!" she exclaimed. She started to hum something unrecognizable and a bit too cheery for my current mood under her breath as she locked the bathroom stall behind her. Fumbling to grab my things and get out of there as soon as possible in order to avoid an awkward conversation, I heard her speak from the other side of the stall.

"It wasn't as bad as you think you know!" My eyes grew wide. *What? How did she … ?*

And then silence for a few moments as, I'm assuming, she was finishing her business.

When she opened that bathroom stall door, she did it as if she was about to give her opening monologue on stage in a theater full of a thousand people. "I was there, and it wasn't that bad."

"Excuse me?" I replied. "You were where?"

"In the auditorium, listening to your research. We've been so excited since we heard you were coming, and I wanted to see for myself if all the rumors were true."

Christ. People already knew I was bad at this before I got here?

"Rumors?"

"Yes silly girl, about your brilliance. And, I must say, the rumors were accurate indeed."

I turned toward my reflection and swiftly moved my gaze to the floor, a bit gobsmacked by what she said, as I obviously wasn't expecting it. "It definitely didn't feel brilliant. I didn't even get any sort of reaction when it was over."

She walked over to me and put her right hand under my chin to tilt my head up so my eyes were looking directly into hers. A very brazen thing to do to a stranger but, to my surprise, I let her.

"It doesn't matter if they didn't react. These kids have so much going through their minds they can barely think straight, let alone react properly to a presentation. Obviously, the research was well done and you presented it well, but let me ask you a question. Did you believe it? Did you believe anything you said up there?"

"I'm not sure," came out of my mouth far more quickly than I anticipated. "I mean, I thought I did, until it was over, and now I'm not sure if I ever did."

She dropped her hand from my face and, to my shock and horror, began to laugh. The next thing I knew she was fumbling around in a handbag that had to be at least half her size. She started frantically removing miscellaneous objects from it. All of a sudden, there were bits of paper flying in the air and I swear I saw at least three pairs of glasses getting tossed onto the counter. I couldn't do anything but watch as she flung her belongings onto every surface and her arm seemed to simultaneously disappear into the bottom of the bag. A look of frustration grew on her face until the moment she seemed to have finally found what she was looking for. Her arm raised slowly out of the ginormous purse until she had only a single item between her fingers. " Aha! I knew I held onto this for a reason."

She handed over the object, which appeared to be an old and tattered business card. Creased and worn from being in the bottom of that sack for what might be 100 years, I realized I couldn't even make out the words on it.

"It's down the bottom of Trinity Street," she exclaimed.

I narrowed my eyes to get a closer look, to see if there was anything still legible that might clue me into what this place actually was that she was recommending. The only thing I could read was the name "AL's." There was no address, no phone number, nothing. I opened my handbook and began digging for a pen to write the location she mentioned on the back. I looked up to ask her if she could tell me the building number, but before I could I heard the gentle thud of the bathroom door closing. As quickly as she'd come in, she was gone.

I gathered my things and shoved the card into the bottom of my own purse.

I guess, like everything else, I'll have to figure it out myself.

I'd love to say that I didn't know what I'd be walking out to when I left the building, but as I looked out the windows on my way outside, I could see just how much the weather was a reflection of my current state of mind. With a heavy sigh, I grabbed my umbrella from the basket by the door, pulled the hood of my oversized coat over my head, and walked out into a typical grey and rainy English evening. While the weather may not have been a shock, the buzz of the city center certainly was. There were people selling their soaps and their produce, seemingly unbothered by the dampness, most of them smiling, which only irritated me of course. There were others walking by with fervor to catch their trains, probably on their way home to their families or to stop by the local pub and have a pint before returning to their comfy sofas and peaceful lives. And then there was me.

My anxiety was starting to accelerate and my hands started to tremble. I got this guttural feeling in my throat and I knew that what I really needed was to scream. I needed to scream to the world how unfair it all was, how miserable this was, and more than anything, I needed someone to hear me. I also knew at a cellular level that English people don't particularly enjoy that type of drama, so I commanded myself to swallow it. I just needed to walk it off. My brain kept telling me to just go back to the hotel and lay down, that maybe sleep would provide some clarity. But my heart … my heart told me to keep walking.

As I forced myself to put one foot in front of another on the ancient cobblestones, memories started to flood my brain. Memories of a childhood full of books, and sleepless nights reading with a flashlight under my bed covers. Books with pictures of Cambridge and the glorious and regal streets of England that I knew were calling me. I remember, as a child, being so very sure that I was meant for all of this. I've been drawn to history as long as I can recall. Yet, I'm finally here, with the stained-glass windows of St Michael's in my peripheral vision, and I feel nothing but dread. As hard as I try to listen, try to hear that voice that pulled me to all of this so long ago, I can't hear it.

One thing I have always loved about the English was that their shops all closed at 5 p.m. It seems a nice thing for people to have some sort of healthy work/ life balance. Unfortunately for me, it also meant that nothing would be open, and I was walking to nowhere. *How fitting.*

I kept on going in spite of myself, deciding the walk itself was probably the best thing for me. To my left I heard a loud shrill from a group of young kids still in their school uniforms, who seemed to be having the time of their lives hopping on and off the pavement. I felt like stopping them and shaking them, warning them. *Hold onto your happiness as long as you can, kids, because before you know it you'll be standing in the middle of the rain wondering what the hell you're doing with your lives, too.*

My mind went immediately to my girls, Sarah and Eleanor, four and seven. Each of them completely different, yet so full of life. I wondered if this disappointment would cause me to discourage them from their own dreams as much as my mother did mine. Of course, Sarah doesn't really have any wild ambitions yet, only which doll she will put in which part of the house, and which snack she can sneak from the pantry, but Ellie, she is so like I was at that age. A bottomless well of curiosity, endless questions, never satisfied with a logical answer to anything. I wish sometimes I could bottle her wonder and take some of it for myself.

She's got a spark in her that left me a long time ago. It just took what happened today for me to realize it.

I've always been over-analytical in a sense, but I genuinely don't recall at what point my curiosity turned into blind ambition. I went from a dreamer to an over-achiever in the blink of an eye, and somewhere in that I lost the love I had for all things mystical and wonderful. At some point, I forgot what those words even meant.

I was pulled out of my internal dialogue, briefly, when I could feel the drops of rain getting heavier on my umbrella. That's exactly what I need … to have no idea where I am or where I'm going, and to be stuck in the middle of the first tsunami Great Britain has ever seen. Of course, I know the rain's not all that bad, but everyone here is used to it except me. Then again, everyone here has not had the worst day of their lives.

I notice a lush, green, ivy-covered building to my left and take note: at one point in time I would have stopped to drink that in. I would have appreciated the way the leaves climbed up the side of this age-old structure, winding and twisting as they led to some secret rooftop garden. I would have stood and marveled for a bit. At this moment, though, as the rain grows heavier and the wind picks up, I secretly hope the ivy shoots off the building, grabs me into its vine, and swallows me whole. *Please.*

I start to quicken my pace, looking everywhere for some sort of extra cover from the weather. Not only had the English drizzle turned into a full-on flood, it was also bitterly cold. With every gust of wind, my body began to shudder more. I grew even more concerned once I actually looked around and realized I had walked so far while on my tangent that I really was lost, in more ways than one.

Over the road, I noticed an alleyway that led to another street. It seemed to be partially covered and I decided that my

ONE DOOR CLOSES: THE BEGINNING

best bet was to wait there for a while until things lightened up and see if the street on the other side would lead me anywhere familiar. With water splashing onto my coat from my boots from the sheer force of my running against the pavement, I made it to the other side.

Underneath the small concrete covering, looking onto streets that were now barren, I felt everything inside me come to the surface. Everything was blurry. I felt outside of myself in some way, as if this one day had managed to rip me apart at the seams and I was torn from the very fiber of my being. It was unlike me to be this emotional. I had trained myself long ago to push this type of self-deprecation to the side, but, somehow, I'm not me anymore. And all it took was me standing in front of a hundred people and hearing myself speak to grasp it.

It must be after six now, and the elements certainly weren't calming down. I decided to make a run for it, on the off chance, a shop would be open so I could ask for directions back to my hotel. I ran through to the other side of the alley as fast as I could, as I was carrying a heavy bag full of useless papers and a pointless umbrella. As I got to the opening of the street and quickly looked left and right, hoping I would recognize it, I realized I didn't. I made a split decision to turn right and skip between awnings until I could find somewhere that was still open.

I must have taken only ten steps when I suddenly felt an angry gust of wind whip up from the ground and yank my umbrella straight out of my hand and down the road until it was no longer in sight. Drops of rain were smacking me in the face, and I was so cold I couldn't even move. I genuinely thought that this is where I would lose it. I thought it couldn't get worse, that surely nothing else could happen to make this day more grim than it already was.

I dropped my head back and shut my eyes tightly, allowing myself to be pelted by the icy water that was being hurled from the sky, and found myself praying. I didn't know who I was praying to, or for what exactly, but at that moment I was desperate. I needed a sign. An answer. I needed to know where to go, not just how the hell to get back to a warm bed but where to go from there. What do I do when I wake up tomorrow?

A faint sound of thunder pulled me from my thoughts, and as I turned to look around to ponder my next move, I caught a glimpse of a white sign on the shop window I was standing next to from the corner of my eye. I almost couldn't believe it, as I had been sure that finding help was hopeless now, but as I got closer, I realized the sign said Open. I made a beeline for the door, stopping briefly to remove my hood from my head before stretching my hand out to open it.

Before my fingers could even graze the tarnished brass of the doorknob, I saw it turn. The door opened only slightly, but quickly, and from behind it came a voice. "Come out of the rain, child. Come inside and get warm."

I'm not sure if it was his calming tone or my desperation that convinced me to follow the voice so willingly inside, but the next thing I knew I was wiping my boots off on the mat and closing the door behind me.

"I'll take your coat, love," said the voice.

"Oh, thank you," I said while removing it.

It wasn't until I was handing it to him, his arm extended out to meet mine, that I finally looked up and saw his face. I was immediately taken aback. Not so much by his appearance as how it felt to look at him. He was older than his voice led me to believe, and his eyes … I'm not sure I've ever seen that kind of golden brown before. They were striking, but perhaps most curious of all was that they were … familiar. *I must've seen him in passing since I've been here.*

Shaking myself from my curiosity, which could surely only stem from my current mental state, I commented, "I sure am glad you're still open. I was convinced everything around here would be closed."

He grinned immediately, as if he knew something I didn't, and then gave me an answer that I wouldn't come to understand for quite some time. He looked at me through his brown-rimmed glasses and said, "Of course I'm still open. I've been waiting for you."

Ummm … what?

That comment threw me for an absolute loop, and before I could even open my mouth to ask him what he meant, he was walking away from me. He turned briefly, only to say, "The kettle's done, I'll get us a cup of tea. I'm Albert, by the way." And that was it. I was left staring at the floor, wondering what had just happened. Wondering if maybe he was senile, or perhaps thought I was someone else. I would ask him as soon as he came back, because, in actuality, that hot drink was the first thing I'd looked forward to all day.

Still lost in thought, I raised my eyes slowly to observe my surroundings. I needed to figure out exactly what kind of place I'd wandered into. It turns out I was completely and utterly unprepared for the scene that revealed itself before me. If my eyes had widened any more, I'm positive they would have popped out of my head.

It was a bookstore, but it was far from ordinary. It was unlike anything I'd seen before. The unassuming nature of the storefront did little to qualify it as a place as magnificent as this. It was lined, floor to ceiling, with mahogany shelves and colorful books that filled every inch of space between them. There were rows upon rows of bookshelves that intertwined with staircases that led you to floors with even more books. There were little end tables lit dimly by oil lamps and forest green leather chairs dappled around the room, just begging you to take a seat. *This place has to be absolutely ancient,* I thought. I could only imagine what was inside all of this binding.

I had an impulse to run over and start grabbing books off shelves and devouring the contents until I passed out. It was absolutely exhilarating. I knew I needed to get closer, so I inhaled deeply and, as I took the two steps down from the doorway onto the shop floor, it was the aroma that suddenly overtook me. It smelled like leather and cedar, parchment, and maybe a bit of tobacco, and it was intoxicating. It was like I'd stepped into a parallel universe, one that was older than I could even comprehend. I was sure Socrates himself would have wept at the sight of it. I wanted to see every nook and cranny of this place. I wanted to get lost in it. And good lord, if it hadn't been a long time since I felt that way.

I walked around the bookshelf nearest to me, and just admired for a moment the antiquity of it all. I ran my fingers along the spine of a book, consequently rubbing off the dust that covered the title. I propped my head sideways to see if I could make it out and then I realized it was what looked to be a first edition of *Don Quixote*. I gasped in delight at the sight of it and then was shocked that I had actually felt joy for a moment over something so small, so precious. I must remember to ask Albert how old it is, when he comes back.

Albert!

I had momentarily forgotten about our funny exchange just minutes ago. He had spoken to me like he knew exactly who I was, and while there was an undeniable familiarity in his eyes, suddenly it was his name I felt I remembered most.

Albert … Albert … I wondered.

And then my heart leaped out of my chest. *Oh my god.* I ran to the nearest chair and sat down, immediately rustling through my bag, searching for the card that Professor Dawes had given me earlier. I finally felt the tattered corner beneath my fingertips and pulled it out with haste. "AL's."

It couldn't be. Could it?

From across the room I heard Albert's melodic voice. "Josephine, I hope you've made yourself at home."

My first instinct was to ask him how in the world he knew my name, but I figured I must have told him when I walked in and had just been so lost in thought that I didn't recall doing it.

"Yes, sir, I have. Your shop is beautiful," I said with a smile as he rounded the corner.

I surveyed him, as he walked toward me with the tea tray in both hands and his cane tucked under his arm. When he had left a few minutes earlier, he seemed to be using it to hold himself up. Now, his stance was completely upright, and I found myself wondering why he needed that cane at all. I assumed it necessary due to his age, but now seeing him walk toward me with no noticeable limp and not using it, I wondered what its purpose was at all. Does a cane have any other use than to support an elderly man? Perhaps there was something else to it.

Why am I thinking so much about a cane?

"Would you be a dear and hold this for me while I set the tray down?" he asked as he neared the table.

"Of course," I said, gently removing the cane from under his right arm. Underneath my hand, I felt a strange texture on the object and realized that something must be carved into the top of it. I lifted my palm quickly to try and make out what it was. It looked like a tree ... a very ornate, very familiar tree.

He poured the tea and placed a cup and saucer in front of me, and for a moment there was silence. I had so many questions going through my head about this whole encounter that I could barely sit still. I was reeling about it all. *What did he mean when he said he was waiting for me? How did he know my name?*

Was I being set up in some way? I needed to know. The events of the day hadn't really left me with any kind of quiet anticipation. "What did you mean when you said you were waiting for me?"

He grinned softly at me, while taking a sip, which only made the warmth in the lines of his face more apparent. He set his cup down and let out a small breath. He seemed to be in deep thought for a moment.

"Josephine, my dear, one of the things that's always haunted you is needing the answers. I'm not ready to give those to you yet, so for now, let's just sit down and enjoy being out of the rain."

What in the actual hell is this place? And why does he know so much about me?

Wholly unsatisfied with that answer, even though there was harsh truth in it, I decided to keep my comments to myself … for now. The silence gave me more time to observe this curiously fascinating gentleman before me, with a beautiful head of hair, more snow white than silver, countless freckles dotted around his milk chocolate skin, and the only apparent lines being the gentle ones beside his eyes. I couldn't quite decipher how old he was, but with the depth of wisdom in those eyes and the calmness of his demeanor, I had a feeling I was in the presence of an ageless and timeless being.

An ageless and timeless human being who knew my name.

Reacting to my unrelenting attention to his face and surely anticipating more questions, he quickly interrupted my thoughts.

"Josephine, I have a question for you. You're here child, because you needed to be. Why is that?"

"It must have just been one of those wondrous mistakes of fate," I said sarcastically, while my eyes nearly rolled into the back of my head.

He chuckled softly. "Fate makes no mistakes, my dear. And I understand your answer, but what I'm most interested in is what your heart is saying, not your head."

My heart isn't saying much of anything these days.

"I guess that's probably why I'm here then," I replied. "I can't really tell if I know what my heart is saying anymore. Being lost is what got me here, really. In more ways than one."

I'm not even sure how long I went on after that. But I regaled him with my woes of the day, from the failed speech up until the moment I found his door and everywhere in between. I told him about my childhood, and the expectations I faced, not just from my mother but from myself. He listened so intently that I felt compelled to tell him things I wasn't sure I'd told anyone. About how I felt I was failing at everything, not just my career. How I'd been so dedicated to proving myself with my research that I felt I'd neglected my husband and my children, and, in some aspects … myself. I relayed stories of my youth, and how I could scarcely even remember being as free-spirited as I thought I once was. How I didn't know if I ever was, or if they were just memories my subconscious conjured up to make me think I was more human. How there was some part of me that longed to feel at ease again in the world, to appreciate it once more, but that I had absolutely no idea how to get there. I had never word-vomited to a complete stranger before, never mind to a stranger who could very well be a serial killer.

I suddenly felt claustrophobic. I needed a moment to compose myself. I took a deep breath.

"I'm so sorry, Albert. I didn't mean to burden you with all of that. I don't even know you, and you've just made me a delightful cup of tea, and here I am, overstaying my welcome and talking your ear off."

He chuckled.

"Josephine, I know it seems like a lot at the moment, but perhaps if you're willing to let go of all of that, for just a little while, I can tuck it away for you. You can even pick it up on your way out if you wish."

"And how do I do that?" I replied skeptically.

"Well, just give it to me dear."

And with that, he outstretched his arm onto the table and his fingers unfurled until his palm was facing skyward. He pointed to the middle of his hand and nodded.

What am I actually doing?

Carefully, I laid my fingers on top of his considerably larger hand. I smirked as I pretended to place my problems into it. *I'd need a lot more hands to fit all of them.*

I wasn't sure if he was some sort of psychologist, trying to trick me into not thinking about my problems, but at the moment our hands touched, I could feel electricity between them. He brushed his hand over mine and quickly closed it, never dropping his gaze from mine. I let out a nervous laugh at the gesture, thinking he was taking this awfully seriously. He only smiled at me, keeping his fist closed tightly. He then excused himself from the table and proceeded to get up from his chair without a second thought. I watched him walk gracefully over to the rack he had put my coat on earlier, take my imaginary fist full of problems with him, and stuff it into the very pocket of the coat that he had taken so graciously from me earlier.

This is just getting weird now.

I had had enough of the pretend insight and the provoking thoughts for one evening. I wasn't even sure what had just taken place over the last twenty minutes. But I did know I needed to get out of there.

As he made his way back to the table, I stood up and took my chance.

"Thank you so much for the tea, Albert. And the advice. But it's getting late, and I've got to get back to the hotel before the sun goes down completely."

He tipped his flat cap to me as I walked past him, and gave me that same warm smile he had when I first walked in.

"My pleasure, miss. And next time, you can call me Al. Enjoy your evening."

There will not be a next time. I will not be re-entering this parallel universe in which a strange old man in a bookstore knows who I am and convinces me with just a look to tell him my entire life story.

I muster a hesitant grin as I grab my coat, "Thanks, Al."

I'm not sure if I ran out of there, or if my brain was just so ablaze with confusion that I don't remember, but eventually I found my way back to the hotel. I went to take off my coat and remembered the silly gesture Al made earlier: The one where he pretended to stuff all my problems in my coat pocket. I wasn't sure if it was fear or intrigue, but I stuck my hand into the right pocket slowly, feeling around for something … anything.

Nothing. *Thank God.* If he had actually managed to put something in there I might have had to call the police.

I threw my bag to the ground and my coat soon followed. I didn't even have to energy to change into pajamas. There was only enough to make a necessary call … home … to Jim.

Jim was always supportive of me, but I knew there was a part of him that probably felt neglected by the countless hours I spend in the office and traipsing around the world researching. When we met ten years ago, I was different. I was fun. I was … free. But something changed in me along the way, and I'd be lying if I said wasn't scared that someday I'd come home from one of my trips to find both him and the girls gone. *I wouldn't blame him.*

The phone was heavy in my hands and it felt like it rang forever before he finally picked up.

"Hello? Jo, is that you?"

A little voice followed his. "Mom! Is that Mom? HIIII, MOM!!!"

I laughed and suddenly felt more at ease than I had all day. *They were still there.*

"Hi guys, it's me! I miss you, Elly belly! Give Sarah a kiss for me, okay?"

"When are you coming home, Mommy?"

My heart sank. I hated when she asked me that, even though I knew it was only a few more days. The guilt of leaving them would never go away.

"I'll be home soon, sweet pea. Don't you worry."

I heard the phone jumble as she set it down before Jim picked it back up.

"Sorry, babe, they have been waiting all day to hear your voice. So have I."

I knew he meant it from a loving place, but it just made my heart ache.

"Well, I'm here now. I miss you all."

"We miss you too, Jo. So, how did it go today, Miss Presenter? Miss Cambridge University??"

I loved the enthusiasm in his voice, and I didn't have the heart to tell him the truth.

"Oh, yeah. It was … great. A smaller audience than I expected, I think, but it was well received. I have some classes to observe the rest of the week, and then my last presentation on Friday. I'm flying back Saturday morning."

"That's great, J. I knew you would crush it. I, umm, I wanted to tell you that I spoke to the dean of Newbridge when he came into the office the other day, and he said they are looking for professors."

I tried to stifle my disappointed sigh.

There's always something. Always a way to try to get me to be more realistic. As if he knows exactly how terrible I am at this without ever having to see it. Little does he know, I might actually consider it this time.

"Oh, wow, Jim. I might take him up on that, actually." I said it with only slightly feigned enthusiasm, and he must have caught on.

"Really? I know I always say stuff like this, but it would just be really nice to have you closer to home, and to me. And the girls. I know you want the girls to see you succeeding, but maybe you could do that here?"

It's disheartening, you know, to feel like the man you married doesn't understand you in the slightest.

But maybe he's right. Today proved that I'm not made for this.

"Yeah, Jim, that sounds great. I've got an early morning, though. I should get to bed."

"I love you."

"I love you, too."

I set the phone down with an exhausted *thump.* And I'm not sure if it was the fact that I was emotionally drained, or that I'd just run through the streets of Cambridge in the rain for the majority of the evening, but the next thing I knew I was waking up to sun peeking at me through the blinds.

I whipped my head around to face the alarm clock. 7:13 a.m. *Shit.*

I had forty-five minutes to get ready and get to the lecture hall for Dr. Beck's presentation. I was still in yesterday's clothes. I had no time to shower. I locked myself in the bathroom for ten minutes to change and make myself somewhat presentable before throwing my coat back on and grabbing my bag. I slung the straps of my satchel over my shoulder, but something caught my eye as it fluttered onto the floor. I knelt down to grab the object and an annoyed sigh immediately escaped my lips. "Al's." *This damn card.*

Something in my heart tugged at me. He had seriously freaked me out last night. He seemed harmless enough, but I couldn't explain how I felt being in there. It wasn't scary. It was just, different. Like he saw me or something. His eyes bored a hole straight through me. *Or maybe I'm just transparent; an easy read.*

I do want to see if he has any more first editions, though. *No, no I don't. Yes I do. What could it hurt? Maybe he won't even be there.*

That internal struggle lasted all the way through Dr. Beck's lecture and through lunch, until finally I was standing in front of the door … right underneath the old wooden sign that read Al's Bookshop. I'd argued with myself for hours about whether or not I would talk to him, but finally decided that my questions from our interaction the night before needed to be answered. I had spent my entire life researching and finding answers, and this was no different. I took a deep breath in as I clasped my hand around the doorknob and pushed it open.

To my surprise, there were quite a few customers inside. The store's emptiness yesterday had made me feel like maybe it was a failing business. But how could that be? It was absolutely magnificent to look at. I was reminded quickly how stunning it really was. Different shades of old leather-bound pages and floor after floor of overrun bookcases made me feel like I was standing in the Khizanat. How does this even exist here?

Just then, a young man stepped into my view, completely blocking it.

"Hello, Miss. Can I help you find something today?"

"Ummm …" I looked around, trying to find him, but he was nowhere to be seen.

"I actually came to see Al. Is he here today?"

The young man's gaze widened, curiosity filling the corners of his smile.

"Al, as in Al's Bookshop, Al?"

"Yep. That's the one."

"Are you an old friend of his or something? Though I suppose if you were …"

"Not exactly a friend, I guess, but I had a conversation with him yesterday that I just wanted to follow up on."

His body stiffened and for a few moments too long he just stared at me, bewildered, before finally opening his mouth. "Yesterday?"

Didn't I just say that?

"Yes sir, yesterday. Although it was after closing hours, I presume, about six o'clock. I don't need much of his time, I just need some … clarification."

Still staring at me, perplexed, he asks again,

"So you came here last night and had a conversation with Al? Tall man, dark skin, freckles, grey hair?"

How many times am I going to have to repeat myself to this kid?

"Yep, that's the one!"

He narrows his eyes momentarily before taking a step toward me and laying a concerned hand on my arm.

"Ma'am, are you okay?"

What the hell?

I'm beyond irritated now with the strange line of questioning.

"Yes, I'm perfectly fine, thank you. If you could just tell him I'm here."

He removes his hand from my arm and looks up at me, some strange hesitancy in his eyes.

"I'm really not sure how to say this to you, Miss, but no one here has seen Al in more than ten years."

Huh?

"He was a family friend. He's known my mom since she was a little girl. He left a note addressed to her along with the key taped to the door … and then he disappeared. No one has seen or heard from him since."

What the hell is going on here?

As I stand there with my jaw sweeping the floor, trying to process what in the world this young man just told me, my mind starts projecting images from the night before.

I was here, he opened the door. He made tea. He touched my hand. He tipped his hat. He royally freaked me out.

Didn't he?

I was still under the concerned gaze of the young shop-keeper when he spoke again. "I'm really sorry, Miss. I've got to go help some other customers, but if you'd like to stay, we can sit down and have a chat about it when I'm done. Feel free to have a look around."

"Oh, and Miss?"

" … Yes?"

He smiles sympathetically at me, as if I'm some lunatic in need of his pity.

"There's a really great self-help section near the back."

You little shit.

Lucky for him, he's gone before I can tell him what I really think of his suggestion.

There has to be an explanation. Either that or I'm going to have to start questioning my own sanity on top of everything else.

Maybe there was someone else here named Albert.

Maybe he was just a creepy janitor who works after hours or something.

But how did he know so much about me?

I was growing increasingly frustrated at the mystery of it all and decided to have a look around. *Not* in the self-help section. I could figure this out on my own.

After a few minutes, I found myself pacing between rows of books, not even taking care to look up at them, my mind a bustling morass of unanswered questions.

There has to be an explanation. There has to be an answer.

"The answer isn't always as important as the question, Josephine."

My head spun around so fast I was surprised it didn't pop right off my neck. And there, climbing down from the book ladder in the darkest, furthest corner of the bookstore … was him.

Without wasting another breath, I unleashed all of my frustration.

"What the hell, Al? They said no one has seen you here in ten years? Are you playing some kind of trick on me? Because I've got to tell you, I really don't have the mental capacity for mind games right now. It's been a hell of a twenty-four hours for me. And the last thing I need is some old man using me for some three-quarter life crisis."

He chuckled. Slowly at first, but as he continued climbing down it only got louder until his feet were on the ground and he was doubled over in full-on hysterical laughter.

I had half a mind to push him over or start screaming. Or crying.

"I can assure you, young lady, this is not a joke. But that … that was funny."

I'm not amused in the slightest.

"I'm just confused. How can you be here but no one else know? Are you a ghost or something?"

"No, no. Not a ghost. At least that's not what we call them, but that's for another time. I'm glad you came back. There's something I need to show you."

"Yeah, that's going to be a big no for me. Sorry." *No way in hell I am going somewhere with this strangely wise, pseudo-ghost, human … person.*

"You said you needed answers. I have them for you, but only if you're ready to hear them."

A large sigh, and sudden wave of screw-it came over me. I was stubborn, but I was also curious.

He started walking away and around the bookcase, gesturing for me to follow. Hesitantly, I did.

We only walked for a few seconds before he came to an abrupt halt.

Looming over him, and magnificent in size, was a door so marvelous in structure I couldn't comprehend how I hadn't noticed it until now.

Ancient, arched heavy oak stood before me, and I felt like I was staring at a thousand years of history. It was the kind of door that looked like it could withstand the onslaught of a thousand warriors. It had massive iron hinges, wrought by hands that must've intended them to last forever. Horizontal iron bands held the wood together and, as my gaze ran up the length of it, I noticed something chiseled into the top of the door frame. My eyes widened at the realization of what it was: It was the tree, the same one that was carved into his cane. I took a few steps forward. *Open it.*

All of a sudden, as if by instinct or some stubborn will, I reached out to slide the iron clasp to open the door. As my arm leapt forward, Al quickly placed his hand on mine and turned to me. "Wait," he said.

"Through this door are the answers to the questions you've been asking yourself for a very long time. Before we go, I need you to be sure you're ready for what it may reveal to you."

I haven't been ready for much of anything lately. But how much weirder could it get?

I thought back to my conversation with Jim about changing careers the night before. About the empty auditorium after my presentation. *What do I really have to lose by following him?*

I smiled in response, knowing full well that whatever was behind this door wasn't going to change my life, but still feeling an intense intrigue about what was on the other side. With a nod as my answer, I slid my hand over the lock and pulled hard to the left to unlatch it. With a clang, the door unlatched and I slowly pushed it open. I had only opened it slightly when I realized it was pitch black behind the door. It looked like a whole lot of nothing to me. I turned to ask Al if there was a light switch somewhere, but, to my surprise, he'd already grabbed an oil lamp off the table nearest to us and was gesturing for me to go forward.

With the door pushed the rest of the way open and the light of the lamp glimmering from behind me, I realized it wasn't a room I was staring at, but a set of stairs. Stairs surrounded by old brick spiraled down into an abyss of more darkness and curiosity. At that moment, I wasn't sure if I was going to be thrown into a dungeon for being such an idiot or if I was walking down into some sort of time continuum. Recognizing my hesitation, he turned to me,

"You didn't think it'd be as easy as just opening the door, did you?"

I responded only in nervous laughter, as he extended his right arm for me to hold on to as we descended the mysterious staircase. I wasn't sure if it was the haunting smatter of dappled light tapering against the walls as we walked or the mystery of where exactly he was taking me, but my heart raced more with every step. When we got close to the bottom, I noticed a faint light looming from around the corner. *There's either another room down here or a very well-lit dungeon that someone will find me decaying in someday.*

We rounded the corner and that's when I saw it. It was another room! But this one didn't have a door, just an arched entryway that I could tell, before even entering, was completely flooded by candlelight. I let go of Al's arm and proceeded to walk cautiously behind him. As we entered the room, the first thing I noticed was what looked like a hundred glass beakers and jars full of things placed around the room. There were lit candles in every direction, and directly in front of me was an old wooden table, that looked big and ancient enough that it could have come from Camelot itself.

Al allowed me to survey my surroundings in silence as I admired the wellspring of cordials and tinctures and botanicals that lined the walls. When my eyes finally made their way back to his, I noticed he was standing in front of a shelf that held a few curiously large books.

"Is it an apothecary?" I asked him, almost giddily, realizing that my apprehension from a few minutes ago had momentarily taken a backseat to my intrigue.

He smiled and said, "Of sorts." And then he turned around to finger the binding of the oddly large collection of literature behind him. I secretly wondered if I was about to be an experiment *of sorts* until I heard a gasp leave his lips that pulled me right out of my cynicism.

"Aha!" he exclaimed as I watched him pull one of the oversized books from the shelf. He held it like it was made of glass, making sure not to move too suddenly, as if it would crumble. His tenderness with it made me think he was about to hand me the original Gutenberg Bible. A trail of what looked like centuries worth of dust flew out from beneath it and followed him in as he carefully placed the book on the table.

"Give me your coat and have a seat, Josephine, so I can show you why you're here."

I slipped off my coat and promptly sat down, wondering if he was about to show me another first edition of something or if this was some sort of inordinately large book of poetry that he would use to try and dissuade me from leaving my career and further drowning in my self-pity.

"If you could only quiet your mind for a moment," he said knowingly. "I've been waiting a long time to show you this."

He hung my jacket from a small metal knob on the wall and took his seat across from me. He grazed his hands over the top of the book.

"Ever since you were a little girl, you have felt pulled to certain people, a certain occupation, and even certain parts of history. That's why you chose your career, is it not?"

"Well, yes, I suppose so," I responded, skeptically.

"What if I were to tell you there's a reason why you felt that pull? A reason why all people feel connected to certain things? Why we can walk past a stranger and feel as though we've seen them before, why we can travel to foreign places and feel like we're at home when we've never been there."

"What if I told you that you had been there before? What if told you that this book contains all the answers to those questions, and all you have to do is open it to find out?"

I let out a long breath, having held mine the entire time he was speaking. I placed my hand on the top of the book and looked back at him.

"Well, I guess I would say that this is a very big book, and it seems like it would take a long time to read. I wouldn't even know where to start." Skeptically, I flipped open the book to a middle page, half-expecting to find something extraordinary, but saw that the pages were completely empty. *Blank. Nothing.* I sat back in the chair, my shoulders slumping and my forehead creased in confusion as I just looked at Al.

He started to laugh. *Why is everyone laughing at me lately, like they all know something I don't?* The lines next to his eyes curved into a warm, gentle gaze and he responded, "It's not a book for reading, dear. It's a book for living. And you start where all great things do … at the beginning."

I drew in a long, anxious breath and shut the book, eager to find something different the second time I opened it. As my fingers grasped the worn edge of the binding, I slowly started to lift the front cover, peeking over the side of it, like a silly child peeking through the living room door on Christmas to see if Santa's been. I thought I saw the marks of black just behind the cover, so I blinked my eyes a few times just to make sure. Behind it, I swear I could see what looked like my name, written in the most beautiful calligraphy on the first page, but before I could even open it all the way to find out I felt myself moving backward. The room started to spin aggressively, and I was sure I was about to faint. Within seconds, everything went black.

WILTSHIRE, ENGLAND

2500 BC

"What is Stonehenge? It is the roofless past;
Man's ruinous myth; his uninterred adoring
Of the unknown in sunrise cold and red;
His quest of stars that arch his doomed exploring.
And what is Time but shadows that were cast
By these storm-sculptured stones while centuries fled?
The stones remain; their stillness can outlast
The skies of history hurrying overhead."

—Siegfried Sassoon

When I finally came to and the buzz in my head relented, I was greeted by what sounded like wind rustling through trees and the melody of a distant flute floating between them; so beautiful it was almost haunting. *Am I dead?* I wondered if Al had turned on some music or slipped some arsenic in my tea to put me out of my misery. But as I slowly opened my eyes, I realized I was no longer in the bookstore; I was perched atop a jagged rock in what seemed to be the middle of a forest.

I must be dreaming. I must have been so bored by the book he gave me that I fell asleep. *Yes, that's it. I'm sleeping.*

Testing that theory, the only thing I could think to do in the moment was pinch myself. Hard.

Ouch.

My brain was ablaze with questions, and my body riddled with confusion at how I could possibly be here. I was just sat in the apothecary at Al's, and now I'm surrounded by an expansive green forest in God knows where. I stood up quickly, trying to find my bearings, but everywhere I turned I was surrounded by a panoramic view of greenery. Panic began to set in, and the only thing I could think to do was follow the sound of the music and see if there was anyone I could ask about where I was. My plan was quickly halted when I heard the sound of footsteps behind me.

And now I'm about to be eaten by a damn bear, although probably more like a yeti, or bigfoot with the way things are going today.

As my mind began considering on the worst-case scenario, I dove behind a massive oak tree to my left and waited for the footsteps, and the thing or person they belonged to, to pass. As the noise got closer, I could hear what sounded like a female voice. Singing.

"When darkness hides, the sun will rise

We will dance and sing and praise the skies

There will be food to eat and stars in our eyes

At dawn, at dawn …"

Suddenly, I could see a stranger behind a line of trees, carrying a basket. It wasn't just a stranger, though, and it certainly wasn't bigfoot; it was a little girl. She couldn't be more than seven or eight years old. I watched her walk into the clearing and head straight for the tree I was hiding behind. I watched her as her wild blond curls blew in the wind, her bare feet skipping across the ground, and her ragged white dress swaying with every movement. She had a single yellow flower tucked behind her ear and was holding a basket in her tiny hand. She was angelic, ethereal even.

Should I make myself known? Should I ask her where I am?

My inner dialogue coming to the surface again, I decided to stay put. I certainly didn't want to burden a little girl with my problems.

She continued walking toward the tree, and I tried everything I could to make myself smaller so she wouldn't see me. As she approached the tree, the singing stopped and so did she. She stood directly in front it and then bellowed, "You can come out now!"

Huh? Is she talking to me? How does she know I'm here? Just stay put, Jo. Do not move.

I could hear her stepping around the tree and I couldn't decide whether to say something or run away.

Maybe she is looking for a friend.

As though she could hear my thoughts she responded to what I thought was said only in my head. "I am! There you are. You found it!" She said pointing up toward the branches.

I cleared my throat and peeked slowly around the corner to see what she was alluding to.

"Found w … w … what?" My voice was shaking.

"The mistletoe! Every year before the celebration, we have to find the hidden mistletoe on the oak. It's good luck!"

She spoke to me like she knew me, which not only caused my confusion to grow, it also gave me a strange sense of calm, as if I knew her, too. I watched her circle the oak, as if she were looking for the best angle to view it from.

"Celebration?" I asked.

She looked at me, grinning. "Yes! It's tomorrow. Mama told me they are finishing building now, and tomorrow morning the light will hit the middle of it. And that's how we know it's the beginning of summer."

Celebration. Rock. Sun. Dawn. Beginning.

I started trying to piece together the clues in my head to try and make sense of it all, but I couldn't. It all sounded so familiar; I knew I'd read about it before. But it was way before my time, so it didn't make sense to be happening now. I walked closer to her and knelt down to get on her level. "What's your name, sweetheart?" I asked.

She giggled, "It's Nes--"

"Nessa! Nessa!" all of a sudden there was the frantic voice of a young man yelling her name.

As I turned around, preparing to hide again, she turned to me sheepishly and whispered, "It's okay, he can't see you."

Kids and their imaginations, I thought. *What I would give to go back to that.*

I watched him approach and Nessa run toward him. "Cowen! Look! We found it!"

"You did it!" he replied, looking up at the branches of the tree and jumping in the air. I glanced up as well and noticed a huge bundle of the most verdant green mistletoe I'd ever seen.

He took his eyes off the tree for a moment and turned curiously toward her, saying, "We?"

Nessa looked at him smugly and said, "Yes! Well, actually Jo found it, but I suppose I saw it second, so that means I found it too."

I never told her my name. Why does everyone know my name? What in the world is going on here?

I moved closer to the boy to introduce myself, as he looked almost more confused than I did at her statement. I walked slowly toward him and knelt down to shake his hand. "Hello, Cowen. My name is J--"

And just like that, before I could even finish pronouncing my name, Cowen walked straight toward me, never moving his eyesight from Nessa or the tree. I was sure he was about to knock right into me, but there wasn't enough time to move and then suddenly … *whoosh.* I felt lightheaded and outside of my body, as if I was simultaneously floating in the clouds yet stuck in the mud.

I felt my heart leap out of my chest as I realized he had just walked through me. It was the strangest sensation. The sheer force of it knocked me to the ground, not because I was hurt or because I could feel him but because I couldn't. My mind swirled.

Surely I am either dreaming or have been drugged.

"Knock it off, Ness," he said as he laid a hand across the moss-covered bark of the tree.

"How did you find it? Really?" He ran to the other side of the tree, just to make sure she was right. "Wait until we get back, they won't believe it!"

Maybe they're playing a trick on me. I'll just walk over to him and flick him in the ear. He can't ignore me then.

So, I did just that. I dusted myself off and stood up from the dirt. I marched over to him to flick him right in the ear as hard as I could and show him it wasn't nice to ignore people, never mind knock them over. Nessa watched me with amusement as I positioned my hand just right, my thumb perfectly aligned to my middle finger and poised to strike. As I released my grip, fully expecting to hear a surprised, albeit slightly painful wail, I watched my hand glide gracefully over his ear, never once making contact. Not contact I could feel anyway.

My hand immediately flew to my mouth in shock.

She was right. She was absolutely right. He can't see me.

Nessa giggled.

But if he can't, then why can she?

I stood there for the next few minutes, trying to piece it all together. I watched Cowen prop Nessa up to climb the tree. I looked on as she climbed and climbed, bark flying out from underneath her tiny hands. I watched her carefully pull down the branch the mistletoe hung on and throw him down bundles to put in the basket. It was surreal to be standing there, knowing I couldn't be seen, not knowing why or how or what. My mind went back to some of the things Al had said to me and I started to wonder if there was a lesson in all of it.

I caught myself smiling as I watched Nessa climb down the tree. She was fearless—grasping onto the bark and gliding down the tree with such brazenness, not an ounce of fear in her eyes. As I observed her, I also couldn't help but recognize the similarities between her and my own daughter. She had to be around the same age as my Eleanor, and she definitely possessed certain traits that reminded me of her. The way a child can imagine, the way they can move freely throughout the world, their innocence intact. It was like complete ignorance of whatever was surrounding them. No, not quite ignorance, perhaps abandonment, wild, free. *How I envy that.*

Once she was back on solid ground, she gleefully grabbed the basket back from the boy and began to walk. She turned her head toward me and gestured for me to follow. To my surprise, I did.

It seemed like we walked for miles, but the two of them seemed so unfazed by it that I just kept going. I let my mind wander as we continued.

The climate sure is different than back home. It's not hot, it's not cold, it's perfectly comfortable, actually. I might take off my jacket, now that I think of it.

This forest is quite beautiful, it seems untouched. I wonder where we are, exactly.

It looks like it might be getting close to dusk. Either that, or these rather large trees are shading any possible sunlight. Where are we going?

Surely, I'm too old for this.

What did Al mean when he said the book would hold the answers? The pages of the book were blank until I flipped back to the first page.

Oh, it looks like we are coming to a clearing of some sort. Look at those two cherubs, holding hands and skipping through the tall grass as if they were the only two people in the world, having no troubles at all.

But seriously, what did he mean when he said we were all conn–

My thoughts came to an abrupt halt as I looked up and realized I stood at the entrance of the clearing. My jaw dropped in absolute awe at the scene that stood before me. It was a village, and it seemed to come out of nowhere. Not just a village; dotted around and between the bustle of people stood about fifty oddly familiar and quite peculiar dwellings that I made a mental note to inspect more closely later. I could see plumes of smoke and men throwing wood and straw onto the fires to keep them ablaze.

Women carried vessels of water and children ran underfoot in every corner.

Children. Oh God. Nessa! Where is she?

In my excitement, I seemed to have lost sight of the only person who could actually see me or tell me where I am. *Great.* I figured the only thing to do was meander a bit until she made herself known or I ran into her. I cast my eyes on one of the strange dwellings and decided to move closer to the nearest one. I could feel my studies creeping up on me as it got nearer. Spending my entire life devoted to learning the ways of life in ancient civilizations, I knew I recognized it from a certain period of time, but I needed to get closer to it to confirm my suspicions.

As I walked through groups of people, I found myself reaching out as if to grab onto them, just making sure that no one else could see me. Sure enough, no one so much as passed a glance in my direction. I wondered if it would be the same with structures, if I'd be able to feel them or if I would simply pass through them as I did with people. I stopped in front of the hut and hesitantly reached out my hand, hoping to feel something, anything. My fingertips tingled with anticipation as they moved toward the exterior. As soon as they reached the edge, they simply went through it. *Damn.*

I turned around in disappointment, but only briefly before I felt the oddest sensation on my hand. I rubbed both hands together to make sure I wasn't going crazy and realized I could feel a powdery residue on my fingertips. A residue that could only mean …

Chalk! It's chalk!

My mind exploded with excitement. Chapters of books and literary journals ran through my psyche as I realized exactly what I had in my hands. Not just chalk … but hay and water also. *Could this be?* I took a step back, knowing that in order to confirm my theory, the roof would tell the story. My eyes flew upward in an anxious pass and then I saw it. Wheat straw thatched onto the roof, hazel rods for stability, smoke filtering out of the hearth. The white of the walls is meant to reflect the sunlight and hold onto the heat. *I remember all of this from my research. I have touched relics of these structures over the years. I've studied them. I have to be somewhere in Europe, still in England perhaps. But if I am, where I think I am, then how in the—*

"Jo!"

My thoughts flew to the wayside as I whipped my head around to be met once again with the cheery face of Nessa.

"You found it!"

"Found what?" I asked curiously, quickly stepping away from the structure.

"Home."

"Home?"

"Yes! This is where I live with my family. Let me show you inside."

More than thankful for the opportunity to study the inside of the dwelling, I followed her, my heart beating rapidly at the thought of what I might find. I watched her skip into the entrance and, as I ducked down beneath the low setting of the doorframe to enter and began to take in my surroundings, my eyes bounced between every surface in the room and I once again started to tick off my mental checklist.

The floor is also made of Daub. A fire, but in the center of the room. Woven furniture and beds made of wood. There's a quern! A quern means they are grinding grain. I must find out what their other means of eating are. I saw fires lit earlier, which means they are cooking, because there definitely isn't a need for too much warmth this time of year. I'd bet anything they are pork eaters. *This is either the most well-thought-out and accurate re-enactment of this time period, or somehow I'm actually here at—*

Suddenly, the sound of music filled my senses and pulled me out of the mental waltz I was dancing. I closed my eyes to listen to the instrument, knowing it as the very same sound I heard when I first arrived. Though at that time I was so consumed with questions (*and still am really*), I didn't notice the unique reverberation of the instrument. *Bone flute. At least twenty of them.*

I swear I could feel my soul practically lifting out of my body. It was if they were singing my own personal aria. I felt my eyes tightening shut, my shoulders releasing, and my head leaning back as I sank into the melody. I can't remember the last time I let something affect me in this way. My thoughts had turned from a yell to a whisper the moment I heard the very first note. I was so immersed in the music that I barely heard her calling my name.

"Josephine! Josephine! Hellllllllooooo???"

I snapped out of it immediately, though I didn't want to.

"Ah yes, sorry Nessa. I was just listening to the musi—"

"Yes! It means the ceremony has started. We have to go!"

"I haven't gotten a chance to ask you how you know my name."

She looked at me and smiled before walking out of the hut.

Knowing she wouldn't answer my question directly—because no one seems to these days—I decided to just blindly follow her lead, yet again. She led me back out into the village, which was almost empty now, a stark contrast to the bustling center I witnessed not long ago. As we came around the corner, I could see through the plume of smoke that rose from one of the fires what looked like the backs of several people. My eyes narrowed as I tried to look through the smoke and figure out what was going on, but as the music got louder, as we got closer, something in my mind just told me to wait. I would see for myself soon enough.

Nessa turned to look at me, grinning. "It's time."

I followed her as she skipped down the aisle that ran down the center of the crowd to the front where the rest of the children were. Nessa spotted Cowen before I did and promptly ran over to sit next to him, but not before making sure there was enough room for me. Cowen rolled his eyes as she dusted off the floor beside her to make room for what he thought was her imaginary friend.

This is making me think of imaginary friends in a completely different light. Ellie had one for years and we just brushed it off as her having a wild imagination. *I wonder if—*

Suddenly, a deafening silence overcame the crowd. Flickers of light started to dance in the distance, and as they came closer the flickers became flames. Torches, held aloft by what appeared to be several of the older people in the community, moved toward us. At the center of them, silhouetted against the glow of the fire, was a striking woman with long, silver hair. I looked around and could sense that everyone was sitting up a little straighter, eyes fixed on the enchanting woman. She must be the elder. I looked over at Nessa, who seemed to be completely entranced by the woman's presence. As I fixated my gaze back on the makeshift platform in front of us, she began to speak.

"Brothers and Sisters: I'm so pleased to be here, on the eve of a most important event—to share with you the reason for our coming together. As a community, we speak often of rebirth; that was the reason for us settling here, after all. The reason we followed our elders into this unknown territory and built our lives on it. As a people, we know the importance of listening to our ancestors. Of asking their guidance, heeding their warnings, and, above all, following in their footsteps so we may grow as they did. Our community fell on difficult times in the past, but tomorrow—tomorrow is a day to start anew. You see, the solstice is not the beginning of the rebirth, but the height of it. If you remember, brothers and sisters, three months ago we planted seeds. We dug our hands into the soil of our Mother Earth and fed her so that, from it, she could grow. Tomorrow is the start of the culmination of our efforts. It is when darkness turns to light, when flowers begin to bloom, when trial becomes a triumph, and we can dance once again into the light of our beloved sun."

The sound of bells chiming and wild applause erupted from the crowd after she spoke. I was paralyzed with curiosity. Her words certainly were beautiful, but it wasn't so much what she said that struck me. The way she moves … The tone of her voice … Her mannerisms … and those eyes. *Those eyes. I've seen them before … but where?* I couldn't pull my gaze away from her until I figured out where I'd seen her before. It's not like I even know anyone that looks like her. It's her presence. *Now that I think about it, when she speaks she has a lot of likeness to—*

I realized the crowd had once again gone silent. The Elder woman was again poised to speak, but as she turned her head and scanned the crowd before delivering her last words of the evening, her eyes stopped directly on mine, as if she was staring straight at me, even though I knew she couldn't possibly be. At least, I didn't think she could be. As if sensing my questions, an enigmatic smile spread across her face.

"And tomorrow, when the sun rises and a new dawn begins, remember to give thanks at that moment. For even though our lives are not without strife, just as the days are not without darkness, the light is always on the other side of it. We must plant the seeds of our being and give thanks to the process before we can delight in the fruit of our labor."

As soon as the last syllable was uttered, her gaze broke mine. I sucked in a short breath and attempted to regain my composure. *She was talking to me. Everything she said … but how?* First the bookshop and Al and his eyes and his voice and his knowing, and now I'm here, and this woman looks at me with the same discernment. Her spiritual elocution speaks directly to my heart. I only hope I can figure out how to use it, where, and how exactly all this applies to my life.

In shock, and still fighting my emotions, I heard Nessa calling me and turned to see her standing next to a very amused Cowen. She gestured for me to follow her once again, and I couldn't help but wonder what curiosity awaited me around the next corner.

We took a short walk back to her hut, where the family was preparing for sleep. This was the first time I got to see her family unit: two sisters and a mother. She was the youngest, by quite a few years it seemed. I couldn't help but notice the absence of a father figure, but I didn't dare to ask. I observed as her eldest sister put the fire out, and her mother kissed everyone on the head before bidding them goodnight.

I wonder if I'll get to sleep. I'm still not sure how all of this works, but I do know I'm exhausted.

Nessa pulled back the sheep skin from her wooden pallet of a bed and laid a makeshift pillow beside herself. She looked as if she were about to lay down, but turned to me and whispered, "It's time to sleep, Jo." As if we were having a slumber party or something. I couldn't turn down the offer, as rest was what I needed most. *After all, if I sleep, I may wake up from this extended dream I seem to be having.*

I took my place beside her, and it felt just like being at home when I would lie down with Sarah and Ellie to get them to sleep. I lay there for a moment, unsure if I wanted to close my eyes or not. There was still so much to process about the day. All of a sudden, Nessa rolled over to look at me and said, "Can you put your arm around me? I'm freezing."

I swiftly reminded her, "My arm will only go straight through you. I'm afraid I can't be of any help."

She giggled. "Just try it. You'll see."

My heart warmed. She was so sweet, and her brazenness was undeniably endearing.

My maternal instinct was to just give it a try. *What's the worst that could happen?* I closed my eyes and stretched out my arm, preparing to hold her like I do my own daughters, and lowered it slowly to hug her. I kept my eyes closed so I wouldn't be disappointed by not being able to keep her warm. As I shifted my arm into position I felt the sensation of it passing through her, but instead of discontent, to my astonishment I suddenly felt … warmth, like I was being enveloped in comfort. I could swear I even felt the pressure of an arm around me when, in truth, there was nothing there.

It's as if somehow … by placing my arm over Nessa, I'm somehow hugging …

And then, for the first time in years, my mind quieted. I allowed myself to feel at ease. For the first time since I was a child I wasn't bothered by the who, when, and where of it all. For what felt like the first time ever, I fell blissfully asleep without a worry of what tomorrow would bring.

I woke suddenly, to the sound of chiming bells and chaos in the hut. Within my surprise that I was still there, I found myself excited to witness the day's events, whatever they were. In the corner, Nessa's mother was hurriedly placing flowers in her hair that had been pinned back loosely with what looked like small sticks of wood. She was in another white dress, this one much cleaner than the last.

"Come, girls, we must be there before the sun," her mother bellowed. There was an urgency in the air today that wasn't there yesterday, and I could feel the elation in my bones.

Before I could even stand, everyone was rushing out of the house. I made a mad dash for the door and realized as I got outside that they were already on their way to their destination. I followed the crowd of flower-bearing women through the clearing I'd come to when I first arrived at the village, back into the very same woods I woke up in the day before. Ahead of us, the children were singing the same song I heard Nessa crooning yesterday.

"*At Dawn … At Dawn*"

I couldn't help but wonder where we were going. I had my suspicions, but truth be told I was here yesterday and I hadn't seen anything spectacular in these woods. It was beautiful, sure, but not worthy of an entire village flocking to see it. *Was it?*

The singing continued, along with the clamor of instruments held by villagers. I noticed that, up ahead, two men carried a long piece of wood together on their shoulders with what appeared to be a wild hog tied to it. *So, they do eat pork.* I was impressed with my cleverness. We had to be where I thought we were. There was too much likeness to everything I had studied. Maybe I'm dreaming this because it will help me with my research. Maybe that's what Al meant when he said I would find the answers. *Best dream ever.*

Despite being overly pleased with myself at my discovery, I still had doubts. It would be too good to be true, and I didn't want to be disappointed.

I hadn't realized I'd been staring at the ground the whole time we were walking. I looked up in just enough time to realize everyone in front of me had stopped. Not being able to make physical contact with anyone meant I couldn't feel it as I walked through them. And, somehow, while lost in thought, I had managed to walk to the very front of the crowd. My eyes turned away from the masses of people that stood beside me, and I jolted forward at the realization.

My heart stopped. I couldn't move. The only thing I could feel was my labored breathing and tears welling up in my eyes.

There it is. I'm really here.

The crowd was starting to disperse and walk toward the site, but I still couldn't shift myself forward. *Not yet.*

I heard a muffled sound behind me. Shortly after, Nessa appeared at my side. She looked at me, then looked out at the view and gasped. All of a sudden, she was stoic. She just stood there, next to me, taking it all in. I finally moved my gaze from the site to her. She was smiling, and there were tears in her eyes, too.

As the last group of people made their way around us, I noticed out of the corner of my eye that someone had stopped next to Nessa. I heard a quiet conversation between them, so out of pure curiosity I turned to see who she was talking to. I sucked in my breath. It was the elder woman who had addressed the village the night before. I got closer to hear what she was saying.

I couldn't help but wonder what their connection was, outside of the hierarchy of the village. The elder woman was looking at her with a softness that said she knew her.

"I know, my young friend, that you are wondering how all of this happened. How this all came to be." She gestured to the stone formation in front of us.

"Some time ago, your great, great grandmother and I, along with some friends, used very old knowledge to create it. A knowledge that will soon be passed onto you. It was long before you were born, but it's something you already know. You don't remember it yet, but you will …"

She put her hand on Nessa's face and smiled. I watched her draw in a long breath and shift her gaze back to the stones, but not before stopping briefly to meet my eyes with her own.

She knows I'm here.

"Come, child." The wizened and ageless woman stuck her hand out for Nessa to hold.

I watched as they walked on together, but somehow I knew those words weren't only meant for her.

I followed behind them, trying to drink it all in. This image had lived in my mind for as long as I could remember, but never like this. Never whole. The giant sarsen stones were in a perfect circle, and inside them, stones in the shape of a horseshoe encased another perfect circle of unimaginably large stone. It was bigger than I'd imagined. I could have never fathomed the magnitude of it. It felt like an out-of-body experience to be walking toward it. The previous twenty-four hours of my life were an out-of-body experience, really. I'd just given a lecture on this very topic yesterday and felt like my life was over, and yet, here I was, standing in the truth of it all. And the truth was something way beyond anything I could have researched.

The elder woman said the stones were made years ago … that they were made with old knowledge. She never mentioned what knowledge, exactly, and judging by the size of them no one made them by hand because they would have been impossible to move. *If they didn't make them by hand, then that means it was …*

I stopped myself from speculating further. The truth was standing before me, I just needed to listen to it.

As I looked around, I saw that the village was coming together in an incredible display of unity. They all stepped down into the circular ditch that encased the stones and grabbed each other's hands. They formed a perfect, unbreakable circle around the structure, all of them. There must have been hundreds of people. *There must be more than one community here.* My heart delighted at the thought. This wasn't just a place for one group to come together and celebrate; it was a place for everyone. *All the years I've studied Stonehenge, its supposed inhabitants, its purpose … I could never have imagined this.*

I felt my feet moving forward, and I wasn't sure if it was a conscious decision or if it had something to do with the undeniable pull I felt. My bones were aching with anticipation to be closer to it. To touch it. To feel the magnanimous energy that seemed to radiate, not just from the structure but from the people around it.

I walked further and eventually slid right through the entangled hands of the circle. I was unnoticed, except for a few. But I couldn't see anyone now, I could only see what was ahead of me. Before I knew it, I was face to face with the center stone. Wind-blown hair strewn across my face, my heart pumping out of my chest, I reached for it. *Please let me be able feel it.*

At the same moment I decided to stretch out my arm … I felt it, but not the stone. I felt a creeping warmth on the back of my legs and, as I looked down, I saw the light from it.

The sun.

This was the moment everyone was here for, what I believed I was here for. Without a second thought, I fell to my knees. I wanted to watch the sun climb the sarsen and watch the seasons change with my own eyes. It had been a while since I let myself truly focus on just one thing, since I didn't feel the burdens of everyday life heavy on my shoulders, since I felt I belonged some-where. But here, surrounded by strangers, watching this unimag-inable part of history unfold, I felt … home.

I wondered if the knowledge the elder woman spoke of, that resulted in the making of this, was also the reason for the energy it evoked. I felt outside of myself. The sun was climbing the rock like a vine climbs a trellis, slowly, but beautifully. And so, I sat, for what may have been hours, but felt like mere minutes. Tears streamed down my cheeks in rivers as I watched it rise. There were several moments that I closed my eyes and measured the sun's progress by where the warmth landed on me.

As it crept toward the center, I stole a glance to find Nessa. I spotted her angelic face in the line and could see that she was crying, too. She moved her head to look at me and gave a small, knowing nod. I glanced up to see the sun was about to be positioned directly in the center of it all, and held my breath in anticipation of what this meant for the community.

A striking whisper of the bone flute struck up suddenly behind me. It was quiet at first, but grew louder and louder as each second passed until ...

Ding

The bells. I whipped my head back in the other direction to see everyone's hands released from each other and holding a bell. I watched, as one-by-one they rang their bells, seeming to signify a countdown do the official solstice ... symbolizing each individual's involvement, each person's gratitude for this moment.

As the line of villagers got down to the last person, anticipation was in the air. *What happens next?* My mind was ablaze, yet again.

The last chime signaled and, in unison, the community bowed to the stones.

As if the hour's long silence had never occurred, they started climbing out of the trenches and cheering. I watched as everyone hugged their friends and family, kids jumping up and down, grown adults whooping and hollering and clapping out of pure merriment. To the ordinary person, it might seem like a lot of celebration for such a small thing. But as the instruments struck up again and a haunting aria turned to a joyous melody, I understood why this mattered … Why all of it did.

I need to find Nessa.

I turned my attention to locating her and started to run. I needed to share this moment with someone, and I knew it needed to be her. My cheeks were sore from the smile that was plastered on my face, and I felt desperate for her company and to share with her this solace that seems to have come over me.

"Nessa! Nessa!!!!" I shouted until I no longer had the breath to continue. As soon as I stopped to take a moment, I spotted her in the distance. Then I heard her yell back to me, "Jo! Come join us!"

As I ran toward her, I realized she was already celebrating. Her white dress swaying back and forth, the flowers in hair bouncing from side to side; she was dancing wildly in a circle with the other children, relentlessly giggling and smiling, the absolute picture of freedom and gaiety.

I wanted nothing more than to join them … to, for once, live well and truly in the moment. And so I did. And even though only she knew I was there, I felt like a part of it all. I danced with an abandon that I never remembered having inside of me. I looked up at the sky, and laughed and laughed until I couldn't breathe.

Dawn became noon, became late afternoon, and moved toward dusk. It had been a full day of celebration. Food, fires, singing, and dancing were all still taking place. I finally felt myself beginning to get tired. It had felt so good to finally let loose, to just … be. Nessa came and sat beside me. I still had questions, but I knew in this moment that the answers might not come to me. I could wake up from this any moment.

I saw her reach for my hand, and though I knew she couldn't grab it, I let her pretend. As she intertwined her fingers with the spirit of me, I felt it again. The same feeling as the night before. I could see that we weren't physically touching, but I could feel her hand in mine. If I closed my eyes, I would not know the difference.

I turned to look at her in shock. Her face told me she already knew the answer.

"Why can I feel you and nothing else?

She smiled sweetly, taking the small, yellow flower tucked behind her ear and placing it my hand.

"If I tell you, do you promise not to forget me?"

I don't think I could forget this dream, even if I tried.

"Nessa, I promise."

"Because, I am you."

CAMBRIDGE, ENGLAND

1980

My eyes sprang open and I was once again in the apothecary. I shook my head back and forth before touching my hands to the table in front of me to make sure I could feel it.

It's real. I'm back.

I looked around and saw Al's back facing me. The book he had shown me before was no longer on the table, but in his hands as he reached up to place it back on the shelf. He turned around and saw me looking at him, but his expression never changed. It was warm, it was knowing. *Those eyes.*

His nonchalant attitude only perplexed me more.

"Al?"

"Yes, Josephine? Welcome back."

Annoying.

"What the hell was that? Did you drug me? Knock me out? I was dreaming, right? That was just a dream … wasn't it?" I could see he didn't want me asking questions, but I had so many.

He grinned. "No, it wasn't a dream. And nothing untoward occurred. You simply opened the book." He sat down across from me at the table.

"How did it feel, Jo?"

I had to think about that. There were so many wires crossed in my brain I could hardly see straight. *It was a dream; it wasn't a dream. It was real; it wasn't real.*

"It felt … happy. I felt whole. There were things I could have only ever dreamt of witnessing. And Nessa … she … she said she was me. Which I guess made sense, because I couldn't feel anyone else while I was there and I kept wondering if that was why I was there. Then I saw the ceremony, and my God, it was the most extraordinary thing. It was ephemeral but I'll never forget it. And then the old woman, she was this … force. She kept talking about old knowledge, as if somehow Stonehenge had been built by some sort of … magic. I even thought a few times maybe she could see me, too. But I'm still not sure. It was her eyes …"

I looked up at him to see him listening intently, but I couldn't take my gaze away from his face. It was even more familiar now, somehow, than it was before.

"Al, your eyes. They're the same as—"

"Josephine," he calmly interrupted me. "You can spend the rest of your life wondering. You can spend every day trying to dissect and analyze your experiences, trying to figure out what's

ONE DOOR CLOSES: THE BEGINNING

real and what isn't. But truth is in the feeling. If it felt real, then it was. If you felt like messages in that experiences were meant for you, then they were."

I sighed at his response. "But—"

Without letting me utter another word, he stood up and walked over to me, placing one hand on my shoulder.

"If you continue to ask questions, you will never be still enough, never quiet enough, to hear the answers."

I pursed my lips together. He laughed at the gesture.

"Closing time, I think," he said as he turned to walk out of the apothecary and back upstairs. I followed his slow stride all the way back up, through the books, and toward the front door.

He'd not given me even a modicum of information, and there was still something I needed to ask. *What the hell? I'll just ask it. The worst he can say is no …, which he's already said about fifty times.*

"Al?"

"Josephine?"

I braced myself for his answer, or lack thereof. "Is there … more?"

"I thought you'd never ask."

You literally told me to stop asking questions. This man.

"So are there more … books to open?"

"No, love, it's all the same book. It's all part of the same story. Yours. I'll see you back here tomorrow at 6 p.m. You can come straight in."

And, just like that, he handed me my coat and helped me into it. I looked around the room one last time as I buttoned it up and prepared to leave. *Spellbinding. There's no denying every inch of this place in incredible.*

No matter how much I don't understand it.

He opened the door for me. Thankful to see that the rain had stopped, I turned to him. "Goodnight, Al."

He winked.

Of course he did.

I smiled as the slow creak of the bookshop door sounded behind me. I stuffed my hands into my coat pockets to escape the chill. I felt something beneath my hand in my right pocket.

I don't remember having anything in here.

I couldn't quite make out the shape or texture of it at first, and then I remembered yesterday when Al had gone over to my jacket and pretended to put my problems in my pockets. I let my fingers brush the object gently, and then it hit me.

I knew exactly what was in there.

I pulled it out slowly, holding it in my hand, just standing there and staring at it.

Small, delicate, and unmistakable; it was a flower.

A yellow one.

NEW MEXICO

Present Day

"You have got to be kidding me."

I snapped out of storytelling mode to meet his gaze before realizing that comment was meant for me.

"No, Mr. Desh, I'm not kidding you."

I couldn't help but smile. I knew there would be only a few possible reactions to me telling that story. One: disbelief. Two: complete and utter confusion. And three: intrigue. So far, number one was winning.

"So, you're telling me, that you accidentally found a book shop, owned by a magical man with a magical basement, and he gave you a book that transported you to one of the most debated points in history so you could see for yourself what it was like, all the while following around a strange little girl who gave you a flower, and that's the reason you know so much about Stonehenge?"

I threw my head back and laughed. I couldn't help it. I expected this reaction from at least one of them, but it made the most sense coming from him.

"Well, Rohan, if I had just said it like that, I could have saved us all a lot of time."

Lucy sat up from her blanket and began to cackle. Rohan shot her a look that could have killed. She started laughing even harder after she saw his face. He swiftly turned his attention back to me.

"So, what's next then? Are you going to tell us that some ancient shaman god is waiting for us at the top of the hill to give us all gold doubloons?" He looked around at the other students, waiting for someone else to join in with his hysterics.

"That's an interesting thought, Mr. Desh, and perhaps. But if we don't get back to this hike and set up camp before nightfall, we may never know. Just make sure you keep an eye out for the ancient shaman god while we're walking. And let us know if you see him." I winked at him, and it made him wince. It never failed to amuse me when I made skeptics uncomfortable. They all come around in their own time.

I stood up and started to pack my things before setting off again, and Lucy walked over to join me.

She playfully nudged my shoulder with her own. "I've been waiting a long time to hear that story, you know. And God, is it good. It never gets old. Unlike us."

"Ha. Now that I hear you say it, I'm beginning to suspect it was you who wanted to hear it, not them."

Her expression suddenly turned serious, her stare intense and knowing. "Oh no, Josephine. There are others."

"We'll see, Lu. We'll see."

"Pip pop, off we go!" she sang, as if she hadn't turned into Gollum just a second ago. And before I knew it, everyone was packed and we were on our way.

We had about another mile left to go before we set up camp for the night. It felt so good to just sit and relive those stories in my mind. I remember a time when I thought they were just that: in my mind. But I've experienced too much now in this life to think otherwise anymore. It was as real as the pines that surrounded us. As evident as the cold wind that was blowing through them.

About a half hour in, I could feel myself getting tired. I looked up from the trail and down at the sprawling wilderness below us. Just a speck of William's Lake was left dancing in my peripheral vision. I may be old now, but the view would never age. *I wonder if I'll ever get to tell them about this place. How it used to be.* A dreamy sigh overcame me. I decided to just spend the rest of the day's hike enjoying my surroundings. I wasn't sure when I'd ever see it again after this, and it's been a part of me for so long.

When we finally came to the clearing, I could hear Lucy shouting at the students from the front of the group. I looked around, and the sight of it made my heart flutter. Fluffy white dandelions and powdery blue forget-me-nots blanketed the ground. The last rays of the day's sun shone perfectly on the only flat ground this hike had to offer.

"Find whatever looks good and set it up there! And don't ask me for help, I'm too old!"

A childish grin spread across my lips. She was always funny, but somehow in her later years she became even more hilarious. I watched her as she looked around to find a spot to put our stuff down. I'm not sure what it was, but for a moment I thought I saw a flicker of something come over her face. It wasn't disappointment so much as it seemed to be … sadness? Just the thought of Lucy being upset struck a sharp chord in my heart. I'd never seen her sad.

"Lu?" I walked over to where she was standing and put my hand on her back while she continued to look down at the ground. "Lucy, are you alright?"

She looked up at me with her big, brown eyes and I almost didn't recognize her. It was the first time in all these years that I seemed to notice she was aging. Her spirit was always young, always vibrant, no matter how many years went by. But in this moment, she looked … tired.

"I'm fine, Jo. I think I'm just tuckered out. Do you think you could get some of the students to help set up our tents for us? I might have a nap before we start the fire."

"Sure thing, Lu."

I saw a group of students congregating around Rohan's campsite. They seemed to be discussing something, and I was almost positive it was me.

"I don't even know why we are here. How are we supposed to learn from her when she's clearly not right in the head?"

"They certainly wouldn't have deemed this educational if they knew what she was out here trying to say."

"I should've just gone to the retreat the rest of the Cambridge students are on in Scotland. That's some history there. Not all this magic bullshit she keeps going on about."

I'll admit that hearing them speak so freely about my supposed lunacy doesn't feel good. But I'm used to turning the other cheek. I'm not for everyone, my stories aren't for everyone. I was about to tell them just that when I saw the quick legs and aggressive voice of a woman going over to them.

"She has more education and experience than the lot of you put together, in case you need reminding. She's also published and speaks all over the world. Including here. Right now. To us. I'd hate to be in your position if her claims were ever found to be true. So, unless you want to appear ungrateful and any more ignorant than you already do, I'd keep your mouth shut."

I laughed. *That is one fiery woman.* I took a few more steps toward the crowd and realized the young lady was the same one I'd spoken to at lunch earlier when we'd first sat down. Cara, I think it was. *I must remember to thank her.*

I cleared my throat loudly to catch their attention before the arguing continued. They all turned, quite shocked to see me standing there. I briefly caught Rohan's gaze with my own. His concerned expression told me he was afraid that I had overheard them, which of course I had, but it had never bothered me before and I wasn't about to let it now.

"Do you think some of you could help put together the tents for Professor Dawes and myself, please? When you're done talking, of course." I said it with a wink and then turned around. I could only imagine their faces. Sometimes I like to throw the grenade in the room and walk away. It's more fun that way.

A group of them breezed past me and began constructing the tents as I asked. They had them done in less than ten minutes. Something that would have taken me and Lucy until tomorrow to do on our own, I'm sure. The ache in my bones weighed on me heavier now, and I was suddenly very, very grateful for the students, no matter how crazy they deemed me to be.

As I sat inside the now put-together tent, I briefly pondered going out to join everyone by the fire to eat. Truthfully, I'm too tired and too overwhelmed to be around that many people right now. I grabbed my bag and sought out my journal and a pen. I've kept one for every year, for the past fifty years of my life. It's the only thing that keeps me on track; reading little bits about my observations and the connections I've made. There's always been at least one a day, but today was different. I'd opened up, I'd begun to tell my story, and for the first time in a long time, I found myself grasping for connection instead of just allowing myself to feel it. I opened it up to a random page.

January 26th.

"I was in the grocery store today and an older gentleman opened the door for me. When I looked up to thank him, I got that familiar feeling. I'd seen him somewhere before. A few lifetimes ago maybe. As I thanked him for the gesture, he nodded as if he knew. He did know. There are people everywhere that know. We just have to keep our eyes open."

My heart was warm again reading it. I had experiences like that all the time. *So why was today any different?*

My thoughts were interrupted by the sound of light tapping on the door of my tent. I saw the imprint of a finger pushing against the fabric of it, and laughed. *She has impeccable timing.* "Okay, Lucy. One moment."

As I began to unzip the door, I was shocked to see it wasn't Lucy on the other side of it. *It's her.*

"Dr. Pearce?" she asked shyly. "I … um … it's Cara, by the way. I just wanted to come by and um … apologize for earlier. I know you must have heard what they were saying, and I just wanted you to know we don't all feel that way."

I unzipped the door the rest of the way and greeted her with the warmest smile I could provide. "Hello, Cara, dear. Come in."

"Are you sure?"

"Never been more sure of anything."

I sat down and placed my journal back in my bag as she nervously sat across from me.

"You have a journal, Dr. Pearce? That's great! I love to write. What do you like to write about?"

This girl is charming. I can tell she isn't just here to apologize and ask about my journal, she has more important questions lingering beneath her nervous rambling.

"I write about all sorts of things, mostly connections I make with people. Observations of the day, things I find most interesting. What do you write about in yours?"

"Oh. I … well, right now it's mostly full of dissertation topics. Not as interesting, I know."

I smirked. *I remember those days.*

"What kinds of things do you find interesting, Cara?"

"Well. I umm … I'm still figuring that out. I have a lot of interests, and I know I need to focus on just one. At least that's what my mother tells me. But I can't just pick one part of history that appeals to me or just one event because they all kind of …"

"Draw you in?" I finished the sentence for her. *I hope that's the answer.*

"Exactly. It's like I can't pick just one thing because I want to know everything about all of it. Like when you were talking about experiencing history earlier. I felt that. I'm just not sure I know how to."

"I didn't know either at first, Cara. Hell, I didn't even know it was possible, and sometimes I still question it."

"Do you question whether or not it was all real or whether it's maybe just … in your head?"

She looked down at the ground, nervous for the answer and scared the question would offend me.

"It will always seem difficult to believe to those who aren't open to it. I was the biggest skeptic there was. Even more than Mr. Desh … . Well, maybe not that bad."

She laughed and it seemed to lighten the air in the tent. "He's terrible, isn't he?!"

"Haha. I don't think terrible is the word. Just … closed off, I think."

Something in her face told me she had a much less tactful way of describing him swirling around in her brain. She hesitated for a moment, and then met my eyes once again.

"So, how do you know then? That it's all … real?"

I took a deep breath and smiled at her. I knew what I had to do. *I need to remember to get my journal back out later, seems like I'll have something to write about after all.*

She searched my face for my answers, but there was only one way to tell her. It was the only answer I could give and I didn't have words for it. I reached my hand into my bag and had to hold back a small laugh. Remembering how Lucy had done very similar to me in the bathroom of Cambridge all those years ago, I pulled out some random receipts, an inhaler, an extra pair of glasses, some vitamin bottles, some tissues, and probably twenty other things before I found it.

Cara watched with an expression that said she was sure I'd absolutely lost my mind. I squealed as my fingers finally grazed the familiarly tattered edges of the object. "Aha! There it is. I knew I kept it in here for a reason."

"Give me your hand, child."

She reached out her arm to me and I delicately placed it in her palm.

I watched as she closed her hand around it and pulled it toward her. As she unfurled her fingers and brought it to her face to read, I could see in her body language that she knew. She knew exactly what it was.

She gasped and looked up at me as she tried to fight back tears. She repeated the words on the front of that old business card.

"Al's Bookshop."

I met her gaze, and I instantly felt that connection I'd been missing. Her intrigue, her courage to open the door and ask hard questions, the fact that she wanted the answers. She was it. After all these years of searching, after spending the last few thinking this whole journey was reaching an end. It turns out, this is just the beginning.

A MESSAGE FROM THE AUTHOR:

Thank you so much for reading!

I hope you come away from this with more questions than you have answers because the story of Jo, Al, Lucy, Cara, and Mr. Desh is only the beginning of what promises to be a series full of connections, truth, and surprises.

Keep your eyes, ears and hearts open for book two in the *"One Door Closes"* series.

And remember; it is only when we are quiet enough to hear the whispers of truth that live around us that we will start to hear them.

- J.